FANTASY

THE RABBIT TATTOO

SUSANNAH BRIN

Artesian Press

P.O. Box 355 Buena Park, CA 90621

Take Ten Books
Fantasy

Other Take Ten Themes:

Mystery
Sports
Adventure
Chillers
Thrillers
Disaster

Project Editor: Dwayne Epstein
Illustrations: Fujiko
Graphic Design: Tony Amaro
©2001 Artesian Press

All rights reserved. No part of this publication may be reproduced or transmitted in any form without the permission in writing from the publisher. Reproduction of any part of this book, through photocopy, recording, or any electronic or mechanical retrieval system, without the written permission of the publisher is an infringement of copyright law.

 **Artesian Press**   ISBN 1-58659-063-4

CONTENTS

CHAPTER 1

Bagley Smith pulled on a pair of navy gym shorts and crossed to his bedroom window. "Gonna be another hot one," he thought.

He pushed open the window and stuck his head out. He heard the whirring of sprinklers on a lawn somewhere down the street.

He glanced down at his neighbor's backyard. Lying on the bottom of the neighbor's pool was a fully clothed body.

"Oh, my gosh, Mom," Bagley yelled as he ran down the stairs.

He ran past his mother, Helen, who was in the kitchen. "What's going on?" asked his mother.

"Call 911, Mom," Bagley yelled. He flew past her and out the back door. Plunging through the thick hedge that separated the two properties, he dove into the pool.

When he reached the young man, Bagley grabbed him around the neck like he learned in lifeguard class. As he swam to the surface, the young man began to struggle. He hit Bagley in the eye with his hand.

"What the heck do you think you're doing?" spat the young man.

He climbed out of the pool and stood glaring at Bagley. Water ran down his black t-shirt and black jeans, forming a puddle at his bare feet.

"Trying to save your life," Bagley said angrily. He lifted himself out of the pool and wiped his face.

"You're an idiot," the young man snapped. Anger flushed his cheeks and blazed in his pale blue eyes. A rabbit, tattooed on his neck, pulsed like it was hopping.

"Hey, I saw you lying at the bottom of the pool from my window.

What was I supposed to think?" Bagley answered. "How did I know my new neighbor's a weirdo?"

Bagley glared at the young man, then started toward the hedge to go back to his house.

"Well, maybe if you minded your own business," snapped the young man.

Before Bagley could answer, the side gate flew open, and Bagley's mother rushed in. "Are you all right?" she asked.

The paramedics' siren drowned out Bagley's answer. He glanced at the young man and said, "Uh, sorry, I told my Mom to call 911."

Two paramedics ran through the gate carrying first aid kits. "Where's the victim?" asked one of them.

"Here," said the young man raising his hand. "I'm sorry you were called. It's all a big mistake." He gave Bagley a hard look.

The two paramedics relaxed. One, with a name tag reading Brad, said, "Okay, well, what happened here? Give me your vital statistics first." He took out a note pad to write a report.

"My name is Alexander Mondie. I'm 17. I just moved here with my mother. She's at work."

Alexander glanced at Bagley and said, "My neighbor thought I was drowning. I wasn't. I was trying out a breathing device I invented. My hobby is magic. I'm working on an underwater trick," Alexander explained. He didn't show the paramedics the device.

Bagley gave Alexander the once over. He hadn't seen any breathing device when he'd plucked him from the pool. Bagley kept his mouth shut. He figured he'd caused enough trouble for one morning.

"Okay, I guess that's it," Brad said.

"I just moved here," Alexander told the paramedic.

He flipped his notebook shut and put it in his shirt pocket. "Glad you didn't drown, Alexander. Next time you want to lie on the bottom of your pool, alert your neighbor here so he doesn't need to play lifeguard." The paramedics grinned, then left through the side gate. Bagley's mother followed them.

9

Bagley stood there for a moment. He was curious about his new neighbor and felt bad about getting off to a bad start. "Hey, Alex," he called out.

Alexander turned from walking into his house and stared at Bagley.

"Look, I'm sorry. I didn't know you were doing a trick. When I saw you down there, I just reacted," Bagley said.

"My name is not Alex. It is Alexander. I don't do nicknames," Alexander said stiffly.

"Well, my name is Bagley Smith and I do nicknames. Everyone calls me Bags. So, you like magic, huh?"

"Yes, magic is my life," Alexander said. He stared at Bagley.

Bags shrugged uncomfortably under Alexander's gaze. "Oh, that's cool. Well, see you around." Bags pushed through the hedge and went back into his own yard.

CHAPTER 2

"That's all of it," Helen Smith said as she slammed the van door. "Are you sure you don't want to go up to the lake with your father and I?"

Bags grinned at his mom. "No, I'll drive up with the guys tomorrow. Besides, I promised Dad I'd do the yard work."

"Okay, sweetie. Be sure to lock up, and don't buy any fireworks," his mother said. She gave him a kiss on the cheek, then climbed behind the wheel of her white van.

Bags waved as she drove off, then headed into the garage for the lawn mower. He pushed the mower to the edge of the back lawn. He yanked the cord, firing the machine right up.

By the time Bags finished mowing the backyard, he was sweating. He

11

wiped his forehead and face with the hem of his t-shirt. As he bent to pick up the hose, he felt a presence. He whirled around and came face to face with his neighbor, Alexander Mondie.

"Sorry, I didn't mean to startle you," Alexander said. He held out an icy cold soda. "Thought you could use a cold drink."

Bags stared at Alexander. He was dressed in black jeans and a long sleeved black shirt. His black hair was tied back in a long ponytail.

"Thanks," Bags said taking the soda. He opened it and took a long drink.

"A hundred degrees in the shade," Alexander said. He nodded his head toward the outdoor thermometer hanging on the patio wall. "You can get heat stroke working in this heat."

"I'm used to it," Bags said. He wondered what Alexander wanted. He hadn't been very friendly earlier.

"I just wanted to apologize. We got off to a bad start this morning, and well, I'm sorry," Alexander said. He seemed uncomfortable.

"Forget it," Bags said, finishing the soda. He threw it in an arc and it fell into the garbage with the grass clippings.

Alexander pulled out a small red handkerchief. He crumpled it into a ball, closing his hand around it. He then pulled the scarf from his fist. First the red scarf appeared, then tied to that was a yellow scarf, then blue and finally green.

"Wow, pretty good," Bags exclaimed. "How'd you do that?"

Alexander's blue eyes narrowed. The rabbit tattoo on his neck seemed to pulsate again. "A magician never reveals his secrets."

"Yeah, I understand," said Bags. Tiring of their conversation, he said, "Well, I've got to finish the lawn."

"If you come over to my house, I can show you a lot of cool magic stuff," Alexander said.

Bags glanced at Alexander and thought he looked like he was trying to be friendly, but didn't know how. "Okay. I can finish later."

The interior of Alexander's two story house was almost empty. There were no pictures on the walls or rugs on the floor. There was only an antique velvet sofa in the living room.

As they walked along the upstairs landing, Bags thought, "No furniture, nothing. This is strange."

Alexander sensed Bags curiosity. "Most of our furniture hasn't arrived yet. It's coming from New Orleans by mule train," he joked.

When Alexander led him into his bedroom, Bags was surprised again. Alexander's bedroom was filled with bulging packing crates.

"Where do you sleep?" asked Bags.

All he saw was a pile of straw in the corner of the room.

"Oh, I have a sleeping bag in the closet," Alexander said quickly. He pointed to a closed door at one end of the room. "Like I said, the furniture is coming."

"Oh, that's cool," said Bags. He picked up a red sponge ball on top of an unopened packing crate. "Is this a magic ball or something?"

Alexander smiled, relaxing for the first time since they'd entered the house. He took the ball from Bags and turned it into a square.

"Wow. How did you..." Bags caught himself. He remembered Alexander didn't share his magic secrets.

To his surprise, Alexander showed him how to pass the red ball through his hands and change it into a square by releasing a fold in the ball. "That is so cool," Bags said, trying to do the trick himself.

"It takes practice. A lot of magic is sleight of hand. The hand is faster than the eye," Alexander explained.

"You are really good," Bags exclaimed. He was fascinated with the magic Alexander kept performing.

Alexander reached into one of the crates and pulled out three green balls which he started juggling. "Did you know magicians were originally called jugglers?"

"I don't know anything about magic. I've only seen magicians on TV," answered Bags.

"They're good. But I'm better," Alexander said.

Bags laughed, thinking Alexander wasn't lacking in confidence. He bent and picked up a framed drawing of a magician pulling a rabbit from a hat. The rabbit looked strangely familiar.

"Originally, a rabbit being pulled from a hat wasn't a magic trick," said

Alexander. "It was a gimmick used to get people to come to the performance." He crossed to Bags and carefully took the picture from him and put it in one of the crates.

Bags was about to say something when he heard a car horn. He walked to the window and leaned out. His two friends, Carl and Paul, were sitting in Carl's convertible parked in front of his house. "Hey, some friends of mine are here. Come on. I'll introduce you."

"I don't know," Alexander said.

"Come on. You'll like them," Bags said encouragingly.

Bags didn't notice the twitch on Alexander's nose or the cautious look in his blue eyes.

CHAPTER 3

Bags introduced Alexander to his friends, Carl and Paul. Alexander admired Carl's convertible, a restored 1965 red Mustang.

"We're going to town to check out the girls. You two want to come?" asked Carl. He checked his curly blond hair in the rearview mirror as he spoke.

"I don't think so," Alexander said.

"Oh, come on, Alexander. You can show my friends some magic tricks," Bags said. He motioned for Alexander to get in the backseat with him. Reluctantly, Alexander climbed in.

"Magic tricks? Cool," Carl said. He then slipped the car in gear and pulled away from the curb.

Paul, a good-looking, stocky,

sixteen-year-old, swiveled around in the passenger seat and stared at Alexander. "Magic, huh? Is that why you got that bunny on your neck?"

"It's a rabbit," Alexander said coldly.

"It's kind of wimpy, if you ask me. Sort of tattoo a girl would get," Paul said with a grin. He glanced at Carl and Bags like he was having fun.

"Knock it off, Paul," Bags said. Then he turned to Alexander. "Don't mind Paul, he's had his head bashed in so many times on the football field, some of his brains leaked out."

Carl laughed, but Paul frowned. "At least I play the game. Not like you two girls," Paul snorted. He gave Carl a light punch in the arm. He then turned his attention back to Alexander. He rolled up his t-shirt sleeve to reveal a tattoo on his shoulder of a bulldog with large teeth. "Now *this* is a tattoo."

Alexander smiled coldly. "It suits you."

"That's Paul all right, dog boy," Carl teased. He slowed the car and turned into a parking lot next to an old brick building.

"At least, my tat has teeth," Paul snarled, pretending to growl like a dog.

"Rabbits have teeth," Alexander said. His face then drained of color. No one saw the vein inside the rabbit tattoo on his neck start to pulse.

"For eating carrots," Paul laughed. He made a biting movement with his mouth, imitating Bugs Bunny.

Bags slapped Paul lightly on the back of the head. "Cut it out, Paul," Bags said, his voice firmer this time.

"Well, here we are," said Carl. "Let's go look for girls." He turned off the ignition, checked his hair in the mirror, then got out of the car.

"No girl will look at me in this

sweat stained t-shirt," Bags laughed. He followed Carl and Paul through the maze of tables in front of the coffee shop.

"Why do you think we asked you along?" Carl yelled over his shoulder.

Bags nodded his head toward Carl and Paul. He told Alexander, "Don't mind them. They're good guys. Paul's just a big tease."

Alexander smiled thinly, but said nothing.

The boys ordered their drinks, then sat at a table near the front window where they had a good view of people walking by on the sidewalk. The coffee shop was almost empty except for the two high school girls behind the counter and two women with babies sitting at a back table.

"Not much action here today," Carl complained. He took a long sip of his soda as his eyes scanned the room.

"The girls probably all left when they heard you and Paul were coming," Bags teased. He glanced near the counter and smiled at a pretty girl at the cash register.

"Is Sally coming up to the lake?" Paul asked, watching Bags look at Sally behind the counter.

"Yeah. She said she'd go up to her parent's place tomorrow," Bags said.

"Is she your girlfriend?" asked Alexander. He picked up the sugar and poured some in his coffee.

"He wishes she was," Paul snorted. "Sally Perkins is hot. No way she'd go for a loser like Bags. Me maybe, but not Bags." He puffed out his chest like a rooster. Bags grinned and shook his head. He was used to all the teasing.

Alexander put the sugar back on the table and stared at it really hard, like he was concentrating. It slid across the table toward Paul.

"Hey, how'd you do that?" asked a stunned Carl.

Alexander smiled. "Magic."

"Bull! He gave the jar a shove," Paul said with a look of disgust. "If that's magic, watch this." Paul used his knees to raise the small table up. "I'm lifting the table with my mind."

Bags kicked Paul in the leg, forcing him to drop the table down. "Cut it out, Paul," he said.

"Just wanted to show you anyone can do magic, Bags, even me," Paul joked. He then threw Alexander a snide grin.

"Is that what you think?" asked Alexander. His blue eyes were like ice as he stared at Paul. Then he turned his full attention on the sugar.

Suddenly, the container shot straight up in the air. It hovered over Paul's soda. Then, the container tilted on its side. Sugar poured from the spout into Paul's drink. When it was empty, the lid fell into Paul's glass, splashing soda on Paul's clothes.

Paul jumped up from the table, his hands and arms batting at the spray. "Hey," Paul yelled. Carl and Bags hooted with laughter watching Paul shake sticky soda from himself. No one noticed the sugar container settle

Alexander smiled at his trick on Paul.

back on the table.

"I've got to go now," Alexander said, calmly. "Thanks for inviting me along, Bags." He shoved back his chair and started for the door.

"Wow, did you see that?" Carl asked.

"Ah, come on," Paul snapped. "You two are just big suckers. He bumped the table or something."

Bags glanced at Carl. Carl shrugged like maybe he had missed it. Bags wasn't so sure. He stared at Alexander leaving the coffee shop.

CHAPTER 4

Bags got home after five. The sun had lowered in the sky, but heat waves still shimmered in the air. He stood for a moment staring at the front yard. The front lawn was mowed and edged. Even the dirt in the flower beds was freshly turned.

Glancing at Alexander's yard, Bags saw an old push mower by the side of the house. "He couldn't have done all this in a few hours," Bags thought. As he stepped onto the porch, he saw Alexander sitting in a wicker chair, juggling tennis balls.

"Hey, Alexander. Did you do all the yard work?" Bags asked.

Alexander stood, still juggling the balls. Then, he made them all disappear. He grinned at Bags. "Yeah, I thought I'd help you out."

"Thanks, man," Bags said. He hesitated, then added, "I can't believe you did so much in so little time."

Grinning, Alexander walked down the porch steps. "Maybe I just waved my magic wand."

Alexander's words had a strange ring of truth, but Bags dismissed the idea. Magic, like Alexander was implying, only happened in books and movies. "Next time I have chores," said Bags, "I'm calling you. Thanks again. If I can ever do something for you, let me know."

"Actually, there is," Alexander said, avoiding Bags eyes. "My mother wants you to come to dinner tonight."

Before Bags could answer, Alexander rushed on like he thought he had to sell the idea. "She's making fried chicken and chocolate cake."

Bags blinked. "My two favorite foods! Yeah, I'll come. Beats eating the tuna my mom left for me."

Alexander looked relieved. "Great. Come over around nine."

"Nine?" asked Bags. He thought it rather late to eat dinner.

"My mother is European, and she follows the tradition of dining late," explained Alexander. The four tennis balls magically appeared in his hands. Bags watched as his new friend walked away juggling.

By nine o'clock, Bags was starving. His stomach rumbled as he rang the door bell. The door opened and Alexander stood there, dressed in black.

"Come in, Bags. You're right on time. Mother just put the food on the table," Alexander said. He then lead Bags into the dining room.

Bags mouth almost fell open. The dining room, which had been empty earlier in the day, looked like a furniture showroom. A beautiful rug lay under a highly polished antique table which was set with china and crystal. Candles blazed and silver platters held fried chicken, mashed potatoes, vegetables, fruit and cheeses.

"Wow, this looks like a feast," said Bags. He thought there was enough food on the table to feed a small army.

Alexander shrugged. "Mother tends to over do it, but she means well. Why don't you take the chair on the other side by the window. I'll sit on this side."

Bags walked to the chair and stood behind it, waiting for Mrs. Mondie. He didn't have long to wait. A tall, slender woman, with a cloud of black hair, entered the room. She was wearing a long, black dress that swept the floor as she walked.

"You must be Bags, Alexander's new friend. I'm Serena Mondie," said the woman. She crossed to Bags, offering her hand.

She was the most beautiful woman he'd ever seen. Bags shook her hand, but had trouble speaking. Finally, he stuttered, "Hello."

Serena Mondie smiled warmly. "Please sit down, Bags. Alexander, pour me some coffee, please," she said. She then sat in the chair at the head of the table. "Your parents do allow you to drink coffee with meals, don't they?"

"Well, ah...they've never served it," Bags said. He told himself it was okay, because kids did it in Europe with meals, or so he'd heard.

Serena laughed. "Well, I'm sure it's okay. You're not high-strung."

"Right," answered Bags. Suddenly he felt very grown up.

Alexander sat down, and then they all passed the platters. Bags wasn't shy about having second helpings. He thought everything tasted wonderful. Serena Mondie asked Bags about his family and the town.

When Alexander took the dirty dishes to the kitchen, Serena Mondie leaned toward Bags. "I hope you and Alexander will become good friends. I know he really likes you," she said in a low voice. "He has a hard time making friends. I worry about him."

"He's a cool guy, Mrs. Mondie," Bags answered. He was actually flattered that Alexander liked him. Without thinking, he added, "Maybe, Alexander could come up to the lake tomorrow with me. My parents have a cabin, and we're going to celebrate the Fourth of July."

Serena sat back in her chair and smiled. "That would be lovely. I'm sure he'll want to go."

"Here's the cake, Mother," Alexander announced. He placed a double-layer chocolate cake in front of her.

"Thank you, dear," Serena said. She waved her hand over the cake and it suddenly burst into flames. Bags jumped up from his chair in surprise.

"It's all right, Bags. Mother loves flaming desserts," Alexander said. He gave his mother a warning look.

Slowly, Bags sat down. "Yeah, I've seen flaming dishes in restaurants where they set fire to your meal at the table."

"Exactly," Alexander said. He shifted his gaze to his mother. "I think it's time to cut the cake, Mother."

When Serena laughed merrily, the flames on the cake went out. She cut Bags a large piece and handed it to him. "Chocolate cake is so much better warm, don't you think?"

Bags nodded, then found his voice. "Yes. I ... ah, love warm cake." He couldn't believe his eyes. Steam rose from the cake, but the thick chocolate frosting was not melted at all.

As they ate dessert, Serena excused herself. Bags watched her leave, then said to Alexander, "How did your mother light the cake? I didn't see matches or lighter."

Alexander shrugged. "Oh, she had a match. You just didn't see it." He avoided Bags eyes.

"Oh, I see," said Bags. He added with a laugh, "Well, I don't really. Would you like to come up to the cabin with me?"

Alexander's eyes lit up, then he frowned. "I don't do party tricks."

Bags yawned, wondering why Alexander was so sensitive. "Look, I'm not asking for entertainment."

"Okay, I'll come." Alexander gave Bags a big smile. The rabbit tattoo on his neck seemed to hop as he swallowed his last bite of cake.

CHAPTER 5

On the drive to the lake, Bags acted like a tour guide. "And this is the town of Kernville," Bags said as they drove through a small village.

Taking in all the scenery, Alexander said, "It's really like the Old West out here."

Half a mile out of town, the Jeep's tires hit dirt and gravel. Bags shifted into a low gear as he turned the Jeep up a steep road. "Wait until you see the lake," Bags said proudly.

When they reached the top of the hill, they could see through the forest of trees, all the way to the lake. The blue water sparkled in the sunlight. Small cabins could be seen tucked in the trees surrounding the lake.

"The lake looks like Lake Balliton in Hungary," Alexander said with excitement. His blue eyes seemed to reflect the blue of the cloudless sky.

"Did you live in Hungary?" asked Bags. He was hoping his new friend would tell him more about himself.

Alexander frowned. "Um, no. We went there on a vacation. The great magician, Houdini, was born there."

"Oh, yeah? I didn't know that," said Bags. He drove down a narrow dirt road that wound through brush and fir trees.

"Most people think he was born in Wisconsin. That's what he liked people to think, anyway. But he was born in Budapest. His real name was Erich Weiss," Alexander explained.

"I didn't know that," Bags said. He couldn't help thinking his friend was obsessed with magic, but he didn't say anything. He slowed the Jeep, then parked behind a redwood cabin.

"This is nice," said Alexander. He

studied the cabin as they walked around to the front.

Bags' parents, Helen and Jerry Smith, were sitting on the porch playing cards. Empty lunch plates were stacked on a tray nearby.

"You're here," exclaimed Helen. She gave them both a big smile.

"Mom, you remember Alexander from next door," Bags said. Bags' father stood and shook hands with Alexander.

"How was the drive?" Jerry asked as he settled back in his chair.

"Fine," Bags answered. "Are Carl and Paul here?"

"Yes, they came by looking for you earlier. They said you decided to drive instead of riding with them," Helen answered.

"Yeah, I wanted to show Alexander the sights," Bags explained.

"They said they'd meet you down at the lake later. Would you like some lunch or something to drink?" Helen asked, smiling at Alexander.

"Thank you, Mrs. Smith, but we stopped on the way," Alexander said, politely.

"I hear you are a magician, Alex," Jerry said. He good-naturedly shuffled the deck of cards.

"His name is Alexander, Dad," Bags groaned. He gave his friend an apologetic look.

"Oh, sorry. So Alexander, why don't you show us a trick," Jerry said. He handed Alexander the cards.

"Dad!" Bags exclaimed, "I told Alexander he wouldn't have to do party tricks."

"That's all right," Alexander said. He took the deck of cards and fanned them out several times. Each time, he stepped closer to Helen Smith.

"Pick three cards, Mrs. Smith," Alexander said, holding them for her. "Look at them. Show your husband

and Bags."

Helen Smith picked a 2, 3, and 4 of diamonds and then placed them in the deck. Alexander walked around the table as he shuffled the cards.

Finally, Alexander put the deck on the table. "You will find the 2 of diamonds in your shirt pocket, Bags. The 3 of diamonds is in your lap, Mrs. Smith, and the 4 is under your hand on the table, Mr. Smith."

The cards were exactly where Alexander said. Everyone was amazed and started talking at once. "How'd you do that?" asked Helen, laughing in amazement.

Alexander smiled. "Magic."

"A magician never tells his secrets," Bags added. He thought he'd better rescue his friend before his parents asked to see another trick. He motioned for Alexander to follow him. "We'll see you later."

As they walked down to the lake,

Bags was dying to ask Alexander how he'd done the trick. He had watched closely and spotted nothing. Even stranger was the fact that he hadn't felt Alexander slip the card into his pocket. "You are so good, man. You should go on TV or something."

Alexander gave Bags a pleased look. "I'm not ready. Maybe someday when I've perfected my illusions."

"I think you're ready now," Bags said. Then he saw his friends, Carl and Paul, down by the water.

"Look who Bags dragged along. The hocus-pocus rabbit man," sneered Paul. "Maybe he can make the lake disappear."

Alexander locked eyes with Paul. "Maybe I should make you disappear," he said softly.

Bags heard the threat in Alexander's voice and began to worry.

CHAPTER 6

"Give it a rest," Bags snapped at Paul. He turned to Carl who was skipping stones across the surface of the lake. "The girls up here, yet?"

Carl grinned. "Oh, yeah. Sally, Molly and Camilla are all staying with Sally's parents. Sally said they'd have a bonfire at her place tonight."

"Cool," said Bags, grinning at Alexander. "Now you'll get to meet the whole crew. I bet you'll hit it off with Camilla."

"No one hits it off with Camilla. She's the ice queen," Paul complained.

"You don't like her because she won't give you the time of day, Paul," Bags teased. He stretched his arms in the air and breathed in the cool smell of the lake. "How about a swim?"

"Sure," Alexander said. He peeled

off his black t-shirt, kicked off his black tennis shoes and started for the water, still wearing his black jeans.

Bags stared at Alexander. "Don't you want to go up to the cabin and put on a pair of trunks?"

Alexander looked over his shoulder at Bags. "What for?" He then dove straight into the lake and disappeared.

"Weird," Paul said, shaking his head.

"You're the weirdo, man. Where'd you get those baggy trunks?" Bags teased. He pointed at Paul's neon orange and lime green swim suit. "You look like ice cream sherbet."

Paul glanced down at his trunks. Carl hooted with laughter as he pulled off his shirt. "Or a fruit salad," Carl added. He ran into the water with Paul chasing after him, shouting.

Bags looked past his two friends splashing in the lake. He realized

Alexander hadn't surfaced yet. Bags pulled off his shirt and dove in, hoping his friend hadn't hit his head on the rocks.

Swimming underwater for as long as he could, Bags searched the lake bottom for signs of Alexander. He found nothing. When he surfaced, he was close to the wooden float anchored a few hundred yards off shore. He looked up. Alexander was sitting on the float, watching him. Bags pulled himself onto the float and shook the water from his body.

"You can hold your breath for a long time. That's good," Alexander said. His blue eyes watched Bags every move.

"I didn't see you surface. I thought you hit your head," Bags explained. He flopped down on his stomach and let the sun warm his skin.

"You should be a lifeguard. I think the work would suit you,"

Alexander said, lying on his side. The rabbit tattoo on his neck peeked through strands of his wet black hair.

Bags laughed. "Yeah, that's me. Bags to the rescue." Before Bags could say more, Paul and Carl crawled onto the wooden platform and flopped down.

"Phew, the water is cold," Carl complained, rolling onto his back.

"You're a wimp, Carl," Paul teased. He lifted his head from his arms and grinned at Carl. Then, he looked over at Alexander. "Hey, rabbit man, Bags said you have a device that lets you stay under water a long time."

"That's right," Alexander answered. He turned an icy gaze on Paul.

"Did you bring it with you?" Paul asked.

"No." Alexander said.

"Bummer. I was hoping I could borrow it to impress the girls," Paul said.

"I guess you'll just have to impress them with your wit," Alexander said. With a tiny smile to himself, he turned on his stomach.

Paul frowned. "What's that supposed to mean?"

Bags snorted. "It means you're stupid."

"Like you're some rocket scientist, Bags," Paul snapped back. "So Alexander, show us a trick."

"Don't you think that would be kind of difficult out here?" Carl asked. "Like he has cards or something in his pocket."

"If he's so good at magic, he can pull stuff out of the air," Paul said. He grinned like he'd just proved Alexander to be a fake.

"Shut up, Paul. You're not funny." Bags yawned, stretched and rolled onto his back. The warmth of the afternoon sun and the gentle bobbing of the float made him sleepy.

Alexander got up and walked over to where Paul was lying on the float. "Stand up, and I'll do a magic trick for you," Alexander said. He had an amused expression on his face.

"Great," Paul grinned. He stood up. As Alexander walked around him, Paul began to shift his weight from one foot to the other like he was nervous. Bags and Carl sat up, watching.

"So what's the trick, hocus-pocus rabbit man?" Paul asked. His voice sounded less confidant as Alexander continued to circle around him.

"Put your hands on your hips," Alexander said. Alexander's hand not quite touched the waistband of Paul's neon swim trunks.

Paul grinned crazily at his friends as he put his hands on his hips. He rolled his eyes like he thought Alexander was a nut.

On his fourth circle around Paul,

Alexander stopped. He raised his closed hand and with the other, he slowly drew an elastic thread out of his fist. The boys stared at the thread as it got longer. When he finished, he opened his fist and pointed to the small pile of elastic at his feet.

"What a stupid trick," Paul said, his hands still on his hips.

"Perhaps," Alexander said with a smile. "Or perhaps, you are the stupid one."

Paul shrugged his shoulders, lifted his arms and dove off the platform. A moment later, Carl pointed at the water surface with a howl of laughter.

Floating on the top of the water, were neon swim trunks. Paul's hand frantically searched, then yanked them down underwater. The boys were all doubled over in laughter as Paul swam back to shore.

CHAPTER 7

The stars sparkled in the sky and fish jumped in the lake. Bags and Alexander walked along the water's edge toward the bonfire in silence, each lost in their own thoughts.

Bags kicked a piece of driftwood and forced himself to hold back the questions he wanted to ask. So many of Alexander's magic tricks seemed unreal. He told himself Alexander was just a great magician.

Alexander broke the silence. "I think I should go back to the cabin. Your friends don't want me hanging around."

"Forget Paul," Bags said.

"I embarrassed him today, and I'm sorry. He got under my skin," Alexander explained. He turned his face away from Bag's gaze.

"Forget it. He asked you to do a trick and you did," Bags grinned. "And it was a good one. I've never seen Paul turn so red in the face."

As they neared the bonfire, they could see Carl, Paul and the girls laughing and roasting marshmallows on sharpened sticks. "What took you so long?" asked Sally Perkins. She jumped up and offered them each a stick for roasting marshmallows.

"Carl was just telling us the trick you pulled on Paul," drawled Camilla Jones. She shook her long blonde hair away from her pretty face. "I wish we'd been there."

"Well, I'm glad we weren't," Sally laughed. She glanced at Paul. "No offense."

"Seeing Paul naked is an offense," Carl joked. Everyone was laughing except Paul.

"I'm sorry, Paul. I shouldn't have played such a dirty trick," Alexander said. He crossed to Paul with his hand outstretched in friendship.

Paul finally shook Alexander's hand. "I had it coming. You're really good, you know that?"

Bags studied Paul's face. He looked sincere, which surprised Bags. Paul wasn't known for being a good sport about anything.

"Why don't you show the girls some tricks?" He said. Paul then sat down on the log, leaving Alexander standing with all eyes on him.

Bags could tell Alexander was uncomfortable. "Look, Alexander didn't come here to entertain us. Now, can I have a marshmallow?"

While Bags took a marshmallow from Sally, Alexander sat on the log next to Camilla. Turning her face towards Alexander, Camilla asked, "What got you interested in magic?"

"I don't know. I've just always been interested in it," he answered.

Camilla's dark eyes studied the rabbit on his neck. "What a cute tattoo - magic rabbit, right?"

Alexander smiled a slow smile, like he had a secret. "You could say that."

"Can you pull a rabbit out of a hat for me, please?" Camilla smiled. "Please, just one little rabbit trick."

"Yeah, bunny boy, let's see a rabbit trick." Paul mimicked Camilla's voice.

A muscle in Alexander's cheek jumped. His face and body seemed strained, like he was trying to keep under control. "I'm sorry, Camilla, I'm fresh out of tricks tonight. If you'll all excuse me," he said.

Bags called after Alexander, but his new friend didn't even answer. Bags watched as Alexander disappeared into the darkness.

"You know, Paul, you are the biggest jerk," Bags snapped. He took a step towards Paul like he was going

"What a cute tattoo," Camilla squealed.

to punch him.

Paul put up his fists, ready to fight. "You want to take me on, old buddy?" Paul began moving around on his toes like he was in a boxing ring.

Carl jumped between the two friends. "Come on you guys, lighten up." Both Bags and Paul eyed each other. "Bags," Carl said, "you have to admit Alexander is kind of strange."

Bags dropped his fists and stepped back. "Yeah, he's different, but he's okay," Bags argued. "You haven't given him a chance, Paul."

Paul kicked at the sandy dirt. Finally, he looked up with a sheepish grin. "All right. Maybe, I've been too hard on the guy. I'll lighten up," Paul said with a shrug of his shoulders.

"Good," Sally said. She picked up the bag of marshmallows. "Anyone want another?"

Everyone shook their heads. "If I eat another one, I'll throw up, and won't that be magical," Carl said, grinning. The girls laughed, and Bags and Paul groaned at the bad joke.

"Well, I'm going to go back to the cabin and see what Alexander is up to," said Bags. "See you all tomorrow."

Bags walked alone along the edge of the lake. Smoke from the bonfire snaked upward into the night sky. At the edge of the woods, something was rustling the short grass.

CHAPTER 8

The next morning, Bags and Alexander got up early and went for a hike. By the time they got back to the cabin, they were exhausted. They slumped into the porch chairs to cool off. Helen Smith brought them sliced raw vegetables and lemonade.

"I can't believe you boys went all the way around the lake. It must be 10 miles," she said.

"It was fun," Bags said. He reached for the lemonade and poured himself a glass.

"But in this heat?" Helen asked. "And look at you, Alexander. You're red as an apple. Come in when you've cooled down, and I'll give you something to put on your sunburn."

"Thank you, Mrs. Smith," Alexander smiled politely. His eyes followed her as she went back in the cabin. The screen door made a slapping noise as it banged shut.

"Your mom is really nice," Alexander said as he reached for a carrot stick.

"Yeah, she's okay." Bags gulped the last of his lemonade. He poured himself another glass and stared at Alexander munching a carrot. "You like that rabbit food?" Bags asked. He remembered Paul teasing Alexander about eating like Bugs Bunny and wished he'd kept his mouth shut.

Alexander laughed like he read Bags' thoughts. He did an imitation of Bugs Bunny eating the carrot.

"I didn't mean anything by that," Bags apologized.

"I know," Alexander laughed. "You're not responsible for what Paul says and does, you know."

For some odd reason, Bags felt

relief flood his body. He looked down, avoiding Alexander's gaze.

"People like Paul get what they deserve, in the end," Alexander said.

Bags was surprised by Alexander's attitude change. Yesterday, it looked like Paul was getting under his new friend's skin.

Alexander poured himself a glass of lemonade. "Did you know that Eldon D. Wigton was the fastest magician ever? He could perform 225 tricks in two minutes," he said.

"Wow, that's a lot of tricks," Bags said. "So how many can you do in two minutes?"

Alexander laughed. "I've never timed myself. I'm not interested in setting any records. I just like doing tricks that amuse me, like this one."

He pulled a white glove from the pocket of his black jeans. After showing Bags the glove, he folded it several times so it could fit in the palm of his hand. He closed his fingers into a fist. When he opened his hand, a white dove fluttered on his palm.

Bags was speechless. He watched the white bird fly off into the woods. "Now that trick," Bags thought to himself, "goes beyond regular magic."

Alexander laughed. "Brunel White created the gloves-to-doves trick," he said. He then rubbed his sunburned arms. "I think I'll get some of that cream from your mom."

As Alexander went into the house, Bags stared at the spot in the trees where the dove disappeared. "Mr. White might have created that trick, but you just took it to another level," Bags told himself.

Later in the afternoon, Bags and Alexander stretched out on the floating platform. Carl swam out to join them.

"Hey guys," Carl said. He pulled

himself onto the float. "Did you hear what happened to Paul last night?"

Bags sat up, yawning. "He found his missing brain?" Bags joked. He then grinned at Carl.

"It was the strangest thing. When we were walking back to the cabin, a rabbit jumped out from behind an old log and bit Paul on the ankle."

Bags eyes widened. He'd never heard of a wild rabbit attacking anyone. "Wow, that's terrible."

Carl nodded, "Yeah, we had to take him over to the Kernville emergency clinic. He had four stitches and a tetanus shot."

Alexander lifted his head from his arms and glanced over at Carl. "I told him rabbits can be dangerous. Some people never listen." He smiled, and then dropped his head back down on his arms.

Bags stared at Alexander's back. Slowly, his eyes traveled to

Alexander's neck. Bags thought the rabbit tattoo was darker. Bags glanced at Carl. Carl was also staring at the rabbit tattoo.

Bags and Carl locked eyes. Neither said a word. It was like they'd both had the same suspicion, a suspicion too outrageous to even consider. Carl laughed first.

"I'm going over to Paul's cabin. You want to come?" Carl asked.

Bags shook his head. "No, we'll see you all tonight at the fireworks."

Carl grinned. "Paul bought some fireworks last night. He said he's going to show you some real magic tonight, Alexander."

"I can't wait," Alexander mumbled.

Carl dove off the platform sending a shower of cold water out. Bags ducked, but Alexander didn't move.

CHAPTER 9

Near the lake's edge, not far from the cabin, Bags and Alexander built a small bonfire. Tiny sparks danced in the air like fireflies.

"Don't let that fire get out of hand, boys," Bags' father warned from the porch. "The grasses are really dry."

"Don't worry, Dad. We'll watch it," Bags shouted back.

"We're going over to the Perkins' house for awhile. Happy Fourth of July, boys," Bags' mother said.

As Bags' parents strolled off down the beach, Bags spread a blanket by the fire. The fire crackled and popped as it burned.

"Does your family come up here every year for the Fourth?" Alexander asked.

"Yeah, also Labor Day, Memorial

Day and whenever Dad has time off from work. What do you do on the Fourth?" Bags asked. He took a soda from the cooler they had brought.

"Nothing. My mother isn't big on holidays." Alexander picked up two long twigs and studied them. "Besides, we move around a lot. You're my first real friend." He put the end of the twigs in the fire.

"All you need is one like me," Bags joked. He wasn't quite sure of what else to say. He liked Alexander, even if he was strange. He was going to say more, but his friends arrived.

"We brought more marshmallows," Sally chirped. She threw the sack to Bags.

"Ugh, just what we wanted," Bags teased.

"And graham crackers," Molly added. She put a box on the blanket.

"Chocolate bars," Camilla said, smiling at Alexander. "Do you like s'mores?"

"I don't know what they are," Alexander replied.

The girls shrieked, "You've never had s'mores?"

"It's a girl thing," Bags teased, grinning at the girls.

"Come on, Bags, I've seen you eat your share," Carl laughed. Alexander stared, completely confused.

"You take a graham cracker," Camilla explained, "put chocolate on it, then a roasted marshmallow, then another graham cracker on top. It's called s'more because that's what you'll want when you eat one." She gave Alexander a big smile.

"We'll make you one," Molly said.

As the girls started fixing a s'more for Alexander, Paul hobbled up carrying a box of fireworks. Seeing the girls with Alexander, Paul frowned. "Hey, Magic Man, I've got a special treat for you tonight."

Alexander looked past the girls at Paul. "I'm holding my breath," he said.

"Let's just enjoy the night, okay?" Bags said. He gave Paul a frown.

Paul made a face like he was innocent. "I'm cool. I got some great fireworks here."

"Do you have sparklers?" Camilla asked. "I just love sparklers."

Paul looked disgusted. "Sparklers are for wimps."

Alexander grabbed the twigs he'd put in the fire earlier. He waved his hand across the burning ends of the twigs, making them glow like real sparklers. He gave them to Camilla.

"These are great," she exclaimed. She spun around with the burning sticks, leaving glowing trails of light in the dark.

Suddenly, the fireworks display began. Giant swirls of green, red and blue exploded over the lake and dropped gently into the water. Everyone "oohed" and "aahed" with each explosion. The display was short, not even five minutes long.

"Oh, I wish they'd do some more," Molly said.

Paul grinned and took a skyrocket from his box of fireworks. "Now for the real show," he boasted. He lit a match to a rocket. It flew out over the lake with a shriek, then ended in a big boom.

Bags shook his head. "I don't know if you should be setting these off, Paul. It's illegal, and Dad says brush around here is really dry."

"Stop worrying, Bags. I know what I'm doing," Paul said as he continued to fire off rockets.

"Let's see you top this show, hocus-pocus man," Paul said. He gave Alexander a challenging look.

"I don't have to prove anything to you, Paul," Alexander said. He glanced at a worried Bags.

Sparks flew through the air and fell unseen in the dry grasses near the cabin. Alarmed, Bags shouted, "That's enough you guys!" He tried to make himself heard over the whistles and booms of the fireworks. "Something's going to catch on fire."

Paul ignored Bags. "Watch this," he yelled. He tossed a handful of firecrackers and rockets into the fire.

The firecrackers exploded, sounding like a hundred gun shots. The rockets burst into flame, throwing smoke and sparks in every direction. The girls jumped up from the blanket, yelling and flicking sparks from their clothes.

"Fire," Bags shouted. He started to run towards the burning grass leading to the cabin. A light breeze came up out of nowhere, fanning the fire. Within seconds, the fire spread closer to the cabin. Flames licked at the wooden porch. Alexander ran after Bags and tackled him to the ground.

"Get off me! I have to get the hose," Bags cried. He was pushing Alexander.

"There's no time for a hose," Alexander said, struggling with Bags. The rabbit tattoo on his neck pulsed again like a heartbeat.

"The cabin is going to catch on fire," Bags argued.

Before Bags could stand, Alexander leapt into the flaming grasses. He spun around and around, faster and faster, like a spinning top. As he spun, flames jumped on him like he was a magnet. Within seconds, the fire blazed only his body.

"Alexander," Bags cried. He wanted to help his friend, but Carl and Paul held him back.

"You can't do anything for him," Carl said. Everyone watched as the flames completely covered Alexander and created a ball of fire.

Suddenly, the fireball lifted off the ground and shot out over the lake. The ball of flames hovered over the center of the lake, burning like the sun. The ball grew larger, then exploded into the outline of a giant rabbit.

Everyone watched silently as the image of the rabbit blazed in the dark sky. Slowly, the outline of the rabbit disappeared like campfire smoke.

"That rabbit image was the same as Alexander's tattoo," Carl said. His voice was full of disbelief. Bags nodded but was too stunned to speak.

"Boy, how'd he do that?" Paul asked. He spoke softly, like he couldn't believe it either.

"Magic, Paul. He used magic," Bags snapped angrily. "If Paul hadn't brought those fireworks, Alexander would still be here," thought Bags. He could hear his parents and the other parents yelling as they came running.

Bags stumbled toward the cabin. The porch was unharmed. Tears rolled down his cheeks as he turned and looked out at the lake. "Goodbye, my friend," Bags whispered. "That was some trick."

Nearby, an owl screeched as a rabbit hopped to the edge of the tree line. The rabbit hesitated, its pale blue eyes watchful. Then it disappeared into the woods.

Artesian Press

High Interest...Easy Reading

Multicultural Read-Alongs

Standing Tall Mystery Series

Mystery chapter books that portray young ethnic Americans as they meet challenges, solve puzzles, and arrive at solutions. By doing the right thing the mystery falls away and they are revealed to have been...Standing Tall!

Set 1	Book	Cassette	CD
Don't Look Now or Ever			
	1-58659-084-7	1-58659-094-4	1-58659-266-1
Ghost Biker	1-58659-082-0	1-58659-092-8	1-58659-265-3
The Haunted Hound	1-58659-085-5	1-58659-095-2	1-58659-267-X
The Howling House	1-58659-083-9	1-58659-093-6	1-58659-269-6
The Twin	1-58659-081-2	1-58659-091-X	1-58659-268-8
Set 2			
As the Eagle Goes	1-58659-086-3	1-58659-096-0	1-58659-270-X
Beyond Glory	1-58659-087-1	1-58659-097-9	1-58659-271-8
Shadow on the Snow	1-58659-088-X	1-58659-098-7	1-58659-272-6
Terror on Tulip Lane	1-58659-089-8	1-58659-099-5	1-58659-273-4
The Vanished One	1-58659-100-2	1-58659-090-1	1-58659-274-2
Set 3			
Back From the Grave	1-58659-101-0	1-58659-106-1	1-58659-345-5
Guilt	1-58659-103-7	1-58659-108-8	1-58659-347-1
Treasure In the Keys	1-58659-102-9	1-58659-107-X	1-58659-346-3
"I Didn't Do It!"	1-58659-104-5	1-58659-109-6	1-58659-348-X
Of Home and Heart	1-58659-105-3	1-58659-110-X	1-58659-349-8

www.artesianpress.com

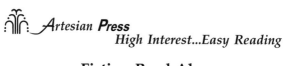

Artesian Press
High Interest...Easy Reading

Fiction Read-Alongs

Take 10 Books

Mystery	Books	Cassette	CD
Nobody Lives in Apartment N-2			
	1-58659-001-4	1-58659-006-5	1-58659-275-0
Return of the Eagle	1-58659-002-2	1-58659-007-3	1-58659-276-9
Touchdown	1-58659-003-0	1-58659-008-1	1-58659-277-7
Stick Like Glue	1-58659-004-9	1-58659-009-x	1-58659-278-5
Freeze Frame	1-58659-005-7	1-58659-010-3	1-58659-279-3

Adventure

Cliffhanger	1-58659-011-1	1-58659-016-2	1-58659-280-7
The Great UFO Frame-Up			
	1-58659-012-x	1-58659-016-2	1-58659-281-5
Swamp Furies	1-58659-013-8	1-58659-018-9	1-58659-282-3
The Seal Killers	1-58659-014-6	1-58659-019-7	1-58659-283-1
Mean Waters	1-58659-015-4	1-58659-020-0	1-58659-284-x

Sports

The Phantom Falcon	1-58659-031-6	1-58659-036-7	1-58659-290-4
Half and Half	1-58659-032-4	1-58659-037-5	1-58659-291-2
Knucklehead	1-58659-033-2	1-58659-038-3	1-58659-292-0
The Big Sundae	1-58659-034-0	1-58659-039-0	1-58659-293-9
Match Point	1-58659-035-9	1-58659-040-5	1-58659-294-7

Chillers

Alien Encounter	1-58659-051-0	1-58659-056-1	1-58659-295-5
Ghost in the Desert	1-58659-052-9	1-58659-057-x	1-58659-296-3
The Huanted Beach House			
	1-58659-053-7	1-58659-058-8	1-58659-297-1
Trapped in the Sixties	1-58659-054-5	1-58659-059-6	1-58659-298-x
The Water Witch	1-58659-055-3	1-58659-060-x	1-58659-299-8

Thrillers

Bronco Buster	1-58659-041-3	1-58659-046-4	1-58659-325-0
The Climb	1-58659-042-1	1-58659-047-2	1-58659-326-9
Search and Rescue	1-58659-043-x	1-58659-048-0	1-58659-327-7
Timber	1-58659-044-8	1-58659-048-0	1-58659-328-5
Tough Guy	1-58659-045-6	1-58659-050-2	1-58659-329-3

Fantasy

The Cooler King	1-58659-061-8	1-58659-066-9	1-58659-330-7
Ken and the Samurai	1-58659-062-6	1-58659-067-7	1-58659-331-5
The Rabbit Tattoo	1-58659-063-4	1-58659-068-5	1-58659-332-2
Under the Waterfall	1-58659-064-2	1-58659-069-3	1-58659-333-1

Horror

The Indian Hills Horror	1-58659-072-3	1-58659-077-4	1-58659-335-8
From the Eye of the Cat	1-58659-071-5	1-58659-076-6	1-58659-336-6
The Oak Tree Horror	1-58659-073-1	1-58659-078-2	1-58659-337-4
Return to Gallows Hill	1-58659-075-8	1-58659-080-4	1-58659-338-2
The Pack	1-58659-074-x	1-58659-079-0	1-58659-339-0

Romance

Connie's Secret	1-58659-460-5	1-58659-915-1	1-58659-340-4
Crystal's Chance	1-58659-459-1	1-58659-917-8	1-58659-341-2
Bad Luck Boy	1-58659-458-3	1-58659-916-x	1-58659-342-0
A Summer Romance	1-58659-140-1	1-58659-918-6	1-58659-343-9
To Nicole With Love	1-58659-188-6	1-58659-919-4	1-58659-344-7

www.artesianpress.com

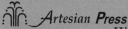
Artesian Press
High Interest...Easy Reading

Other Nonfiction Read-Along

Disasters

- Challenger
- The Kuwaiti Oil Fires
- The Last Flight of 007
- The Mount St. Helens Volcano
- The Nuclear Disaster at Chernobyl

Disaster Display Set (5 each of 5 titles 25 books in all)
80106

Natural Disasters

- Blizzards
- Earthquakes
- Hurricanes and Floods
- Tornadoes
- Wildfires

Disaster Display Set (5 each of 5 titles 25 books in all)
80032

www.artesianpress.com

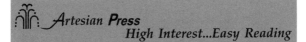

High Interest...Easy Reading

Historical Nonfiction
Mysteries

Ancient Egyptian Mystery Series

- The Great Pyramids
- The Lords of Kush
- The Lost King: Akhenaton
- Mummies
- The Rosetta Stone

Display Set (5 each of 5 titles 25 books in all)
80354